RAGZ-RICHEZ

Crystal Anna

AuthorHouse™ UK
1663 Liberty Drive
Bloomington, IN 47403 USA
www.authorhouse.co.uk
Phone: 0800.197.4150

Published by AuthorHouse 02/05/2019

ISBN: 978-1-7283-8424-5 (sc)
ISBN: 978-1-7283-8423-8 (e)

authorHOUSE®

Once upon a time, there was a young girl. She wasn't the smartest or the prettiest, and she spent her days dreaming about what she would like her life to be when she grew up. She didn't know it yet, but she was a real-life princess, a princess who could help a nation, inspiring and helping millions of people.

A heart of gold.

Every day, school was rough. It became too tough, and she felt out of her depth. So she got up and left!

After leaving school, it felt like she had hit
a brick wall. Life felt like nothing at all.
Leaving school felt like a massive fall!

The princess couldn't cope and lost all hope.

But despite not being able to see
the light, she continued to fight.

She decided to leave behind her home city
and go to Bath, her dream city.

She reached her dream city, but
with not a penny in the kitty.

On the streets and determined not to be beat, she didn't believe in defeat.

Feeling not worthy or good enough for anyone, the hurt motivated her to proceed with her dreams.

Days and days went by. Her dreams were her only escape.
She didn't realize she would achieve them in a flick of fate.

She kept herself focused on a book she had
started writing, Ragz to Richez, her life story.
"Ragz" being the present situation, and "Richez"
being her success through the mess!

Closing her eyes, she fell into a deep sleep
and a world of magical dreams.

It was the night before the official book launch. The princess was on her way in a carriage pulled by three horses; her life was about to take a different course.

They travelled over the biggest hills and through the darkest tunnels. But there was always a light at the end; the princess never gave up on the journey.

Finally, two stone gateposts greeted them, leading to a magical, moonlit, tree-lined driveway. The princess knew she had arrived as this was the special place she had been imagining and dreaming of.

A beautiful house emerged through the trees, standing proudly on the hill. This was the house she had been dreaming of! The lights glistened in the darkness; the princess was amazed. The power of her dreams had formed in to her reality.

The princess stepped down from the carriage and gave her unicorn horses crunchy, rainbow-coloured carrots and a fresh drink of water.

She then walked over to the house. She opened the doors into a hallway. Blue and gold tiles covered the floor. A fireplace at the end of the hallway was a lit, and beside it was somewhere to sit. But the princess had to go to bed as tomorrow was the day of her book launch.

She climbed the beautifully carved sweeping staircase. Three large windows flooded the stairs in sparkling moonlight.

The princess opened the door into her bedroom. The windows looked out over the landscape. The sparkling midnight sky lit up the gardens of the house, and the trees gently rustled in the cool night's breeze.

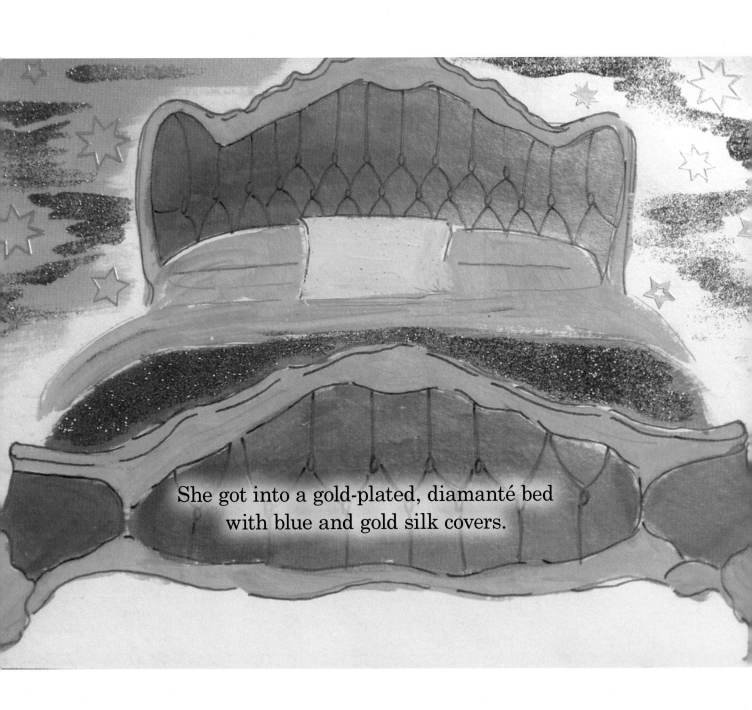

She got into a gold-plated, diamanté bed
with blue and gold silk covers.

After a perfect and peaceful night's sleep, she awoke to the sun streaming through the windows, and the birds singing their morning tunes. The sky was a bright, clear, crystal blue, and the sun was the brightest golden yellow.

She had a healthy breakfast of cereal with
strawberries, honey, and fresh orange juice.

Next she went to get ready for her book launch
and signing. Blue silk curtains framed the stage,
and there were rainbow-coloured spotlights.
The sun was shining, and the sky was bright
blue. And there was a massive audience.

Outside there was a stage ready for her book launch and signing, blue silk curtains framed the stage with rainbow and coloured spotlights, the sun was shining the sky was bright blue and there was a massive audience.

There was a big buffet with magical unicorn cupcakes, millionaire shortbread with gold chocolate coins and real gold scattered over them, bringing "wealth" to the table. There were fresh rainbow-coloured vegs and fruit. And there were the naughty but nice strawberry, toffee and chocolate ice cream; iced doughnuts; and milkshakes with fresh whipped cream. All with a cherry on top!

The princess walked out on to the stage. Love
and positivity enlivened the audience.

There were songs that she had chosen which had inspired and motivated her on her journey to success.

Everyone had an amazing time. Their spirits were uplifted, and positivity filled them with happiness and joy. They now knew they could achieve their dreams if they believed in the magic which surrounded them. They were inspired to go out and achieve their dreams!

The book launch was a complete success! And this book went on to inspire and help an entire nation, selling millions of copies and being an ultimate, real-life princess story!

She owned the "house the hill", the house of
her dreams! A very special magical house.

He was kind, generous, and had a heart of gold.

She was a millionaire, from *Ragz to Richez!*

So, the moral of the story …

Life might seem like endless mould, but if you
have a heart of gold, you will succeed in what you
want! So believe in magic. Life ain't that tragic!

The princess awoke to find her dreams a reality!

Printed in the United States
By Bookmasters